2.9
0.5

To my dear friends Debby & Tommy Thomason—B. M. J.

To my "little" brother, Bryan Sampson—M. S.

For Marcia and James—P. M.

SIMON & SCHUSTER BOOKS FOR YOUNG READERS
An imprint of Simon & Schuster Children's Publishing Division
1230 Avenue of the Americas, New York, New York 10020

Book design by Paula Winicur
The text of this book is set in Berkeley.
The illustrations are rendered in pen and ink with watercolor on Arches paper.
Printed in the United States of America

2 4 6 8 10 9 7 5 3 1

Library of Congress Cataloging-in-Publication Data
Martin, Bill, 1916-
Trick or treat? / Bill Martin Jr and Michael Sampson ; illustrated by Paul Meisel.
p. cm.
Summary: A child has a wonderful time collecting treats from wacky neighbors, until Magic Merlin decides that a trick would be more fun.
ISBN 0-689-84968-0
[1. Halloween—Fiction. 2. Candy—Fiction. 3. Magic—Fiction.]
I. Sampson, Michael R. II. Meisel, Paul, ill. III. Title.
PZ7.M356773 Tr 2002
[E]—dc21
2002070646

Trick OR Treat?

Bill Martin Jr and
Michael Sampson

illustrated by
Paul Meisel

SIMON & SCHUSTER BOOKS FOR YOUNG READERS
New York London Toronto Sydney Singapore

"Mommy, I'm ready to go!"

"My, don't you look scary," my mommy says. "You can go trick-or-treating—but only in our apartment building. I'll go with you! And remember—you only knock on doors of people we know. And try not to scare them!"

Up to the second floor, knock on Knicker Knocker's door.
"Trick or Treat?"
"Treat," says Knicker Knocker as he fills my bag with Candy
Bars.

Up to the third floor, knock on Slipper Slopper's door.
"Trick or Treat?"
"Treat," says Slipper Slopper as she fills my bag with Peanut
Cups.

Up to the fourth floor, knock on Wiggle Waggle's door.
"Trick or Treat?"
"Treat," says Wiggle Waggle as he fills my bag with Tangerine
Drops.

Up to the ninth floor, knock on Teeter Totter's door.
"Trick or Treat?"
"Treat," says Teeter Totter as he fills my bag with Jelly Beans.

Up to the tenth floor, knock on Magic Merlin's door.
"Trick or Treat?"
There is no answer.
"Trick or Treat?"
Still no answer.
"Trick or Treat?"

The door flies open and Merlin waves his magic wand at me.
"Now everything is **WackBards!**" Merlin laughs as he slams his
door on me.

Down to the ninth floor, knock on Totter Teeter's door.
"Trick or Treat,"
"Trick," says Totter Teeter as he fills my bag with Belly Jeans.

Down to the eighth floor, knock on Thamble Thimble's door.
"Trick or Treat,"
"Trick," says Thamble Thimble as he fills my bag with
Stocolate Chicks.

Down to the seventh floor, knock on Pickle Pumper's door.
"Trick or Treat,"
"Trick," says Pickle Pumper as she fills my bag with Paramel
Cops.

Down to the sixth floor, knock on Faddle Fiddle's door.
"Trick or Treat?"
"Trick," says Faddle Fiddle as he fills my bag with Beanut
Putter.

Down to the fifth floor, knock on Lamber Limbler's door.

"Trick or Treat?"

"Trick," says Lamber Limbler as she fills my bag with
Twicorice Lists.

Down to the fourth floor, knock on Waggle Wiggle's door.

"Trick or Treat?"

"Trick," says Waggle Wiggle as he fills my bag with
Drangerine Tops.

Down to the third floor, knock on Slopper Slipper's door.
"Trick or Treat?"
"Trick," says Slopper Slipper as she fills my bag with Ceanut
Pups.

Down to the second floor, knock on Knocker Knicker's door.

"Trick or Treat?"

"Trick," says Knocker Knicker as he fills my bag with Bandy
Cars.

Down to the first floor, knock on my apartment door.
"Trick or Treat?"

"Treat!"

says my daddy as he hugs me in his arms.

"But daddy, look at my backwards candy!" I cry.
"Looks yummy to me," he laughs.

A mountain of candy!
**Candy Bars, Peanut Cups, Tangerine
Drops, Licorice Twists, Peanut Butter,
Caramel Pops, Chocolate Sticks,
and Jelly Beans.**

The power of my daddy's hug had broken the backward spell.
We laughed and laughed, we ate and ate, and we never saw
Merlin again.

THE END